Springtime Treasury

A COLLECTION OF ANIMAL STORIES

PIPPBROOK
BOOKS

Contents

The Bunny of
Bluebell Hill

The Brave
Little Owl

The Blackberry Mouse

Mouse loved his little cottage in the country.
He loved it because it was warm and cosy,
and just the right size for a mouse.

Most of all, he loved it because there was a BIG blackberry bush in the garden

and every year he had a bumper crop
of ripe, juicy blackberries.

One summer, Mouse's blackberries were even
bigger and juicier than usual. He began picking right
away and he was already hot and bothered when
Sparrow came by.

"What nice blackberries. May I have some?"
chirped Sparrow.
"They're all mine," said Mouse. "Go away!"
"No need to be rude," said the little bird,
and she flew away.

Mouse's paws were beginning to ache from
all the hard work when he caught sight of Squirrel.
"Can I have some of those juicy blackberries?"
Squirrel asked.
"If I give you some there will be less for me!"
Mouse replied. So Squirrel went away empty-handed.

Mouse had stopped to have a rest when Rabbit
came hopping through the grass.

"Those blackberries look delicious," she said.

"They are," said Mouse. "And I am going to eat every last one."

"Then you will most certainly be ill," said Rabbit,
and off she went.

The sun was hot and Mouse was getting very tired.
Soon he nodded off to sleep.
He didn't realise that someone had been watching him.

It was Mr Fox...

When he saw that Mouse was asleep, he sneaked over
Mouse's gate and crept closer and closer until
he could pick up Mouse's basket.

He was just creeping away when—
SNAP!
He trod on a twig.

Mouse woke up with a start.
"Hey! Those are my blackberries!" he squeaked.
"You're far too small to stop me taking them,"
laughed Mr Fox. "They will make a fine tea for me."

Mouse was not surprised that
none of his woodland friends had warned him
Mr Fox was about. "After all," he thought,
"why should they help me when I would not
share my blackberries with them?"

Just then a strange thing happened.
An acorn landed on Mr Fox's head!

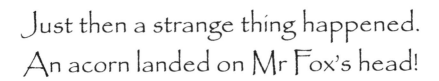

PLOP!

and another – PLOP!

And another, and another, and another.

PLOP! PLOP! PLOP!

Mr Fox dropped the blackberry basket and
ran away as fast as he could!

Mouse looked up to see where the acorns
had come from. And who do you think he saw
up in the old oak tree?

It was Squirrel and Sparrow and Rabbit.

"We couldn't let Mr Fox steal your
blackberries," said Squirrel. "Even if you
didn't want to share them," added Sparrow.

Mouse felt very ashamed.
Then he had an idea...

That afternoon Mouse invited everyone to a blackberry feast. He worked all day to get it ready.

There was blackberry juice to drink, blackberry jam, blackberry jelly, blackberry crumble, and lots and lots of little blackberry tarts.
The other animals said how delicious it all was.

"Perhaps," said Mouse, "blackberries are nicer if you share them, after all."

The Little
Lost Duckling

One sunny morning, Mother Duck led her
four new ducklings down to the old pond.
"Stay close, little ones," she told them.

But one little duckling didn't listen.

"Follow me, my babies," called Mother Duck as she swam away.
But one little duckling didn't do as she was told.
She didn't want to follow her mother across the water.

She wanted to dart after the dragonflies,

watch the frogs hopping
on the lily pads

and chase the glistening fish.

So that's just what Little Duckling did.

She splashed in the water and
frightened the fish. She snapped her
little beak at the dragonflies.
She quacked in amazement when the
beautiful kingfisher flew by.

After a while, Little Duckling was tired of playing.
She scrambled up onto the grassy bank and
fluffed out her feathers to dry.
Around her the wind whispered in the grass.
The leaves rustled, and overhead the sky grew dark.

Little Duckling realised she was all alone.

Little Duckling looked out across the pond.
Mother Duck was nowhere to be seen.
Suddenly, Little Duckling wanted to see
her mother very much indeed.
Just then, Hedgehog came shuffling by.

"Have you seen my mummy?" asked Little Duckling.
But Hedgehog just shook his head, and carried
on hunting for juicy worms to eat.

So Little Duckling walked a little further
down the bank until she met Squirrel.
"Have you seen my mummy?" she asked again.

But Squirrel was too busy collecting acorns
to even answer, so Little Duckling had to
carry on walking.

She hadn't gone very far before she met Rabbit.
"Who are you?" the rabbit asked.
"I'm a lost duckling and I'm looking for my mummy."
"Then you should stay by the water, or Mr Fox will get you,"
said Rabbit. And with a flash of his white tail
he disappeared beneath the ground.

Little Duckling wasn't feeling very brave at all now.
She quacked loudly, hoping her mummy might hear.
"I wouldn't do that if I were you," said a squeaky voice.
"Mr Fox might hear you!" It was Mouse.
"Oh dear, oh dear!" cheeped Little Duckling.
"Please help me find Mother Duck."
But the mouse had scurried away.

Just then, a big, furry beaver scrambled onto the bank.
"Hrrumph!" he grunted. "What's a little duckling
like you doing here, all on your own?"

"I'm lost and I'm looking for my mummy!"
wailed the poor little duckling.

"Is she a nice, brown, cuddly mummy?" asked Beaver.
"Who told you always to stay close by her side?"

Little Duckling nodded sadly.
"Then you'll find her looking for YOU
over by those reeds," said Beaver.

"Mummy!" quacked the little duckling happily.
"I promise to never wander off again."

And do you know what? She never, ever did.

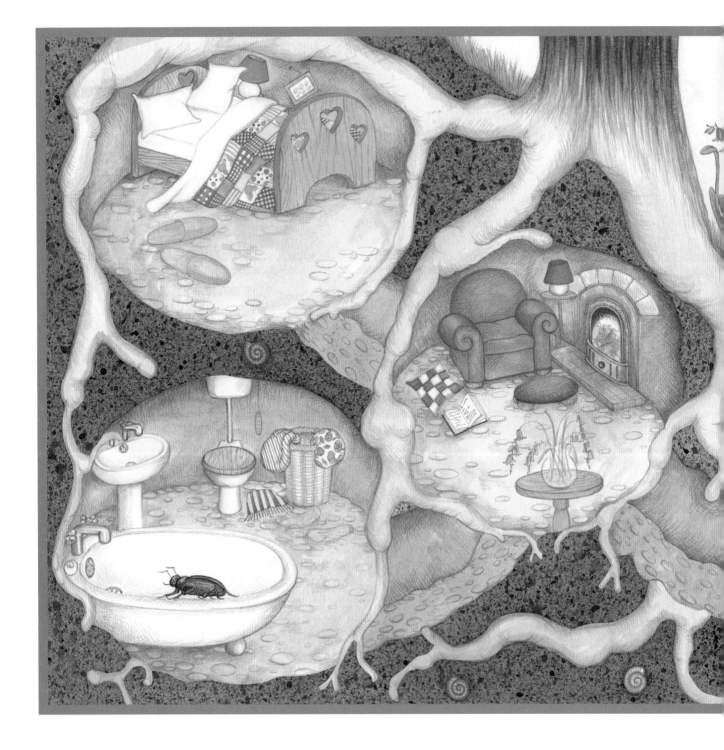

The Bunny of
Bluebell Hill

At the top of Bluebell Hill
there was an old oak tree. And underneath
that oak tree there was a burrow,
and in that burrow lived a bunny.
It was a very nice burrow, with four little rooms
and bluebells growing by the front door.

But Bunny didn't like it.

"I am bored with this burrow,"
said Bunny to herself.
"I am tired of walking up and down this hill.
I am fed up with being hit on the head by acorns.
And I am very, very bored with bluebells!

I want an exciting new home."

So without further ado, she
set off to find herself one.

Bunny's friend Squirrel took her to see
his high-rise tree-house. But Bunny
didn't have a head for heights!
And her big paws just weren't meant for jumping
about from branch to branch.

"I'm sorry, Squirrel," said Bunny.
"I think I need something a little closer to the ground!"

The next animal Bunny visited was Badger.
He lived in a mossy bank in the heart of the
old forest. It was dark and still among the trees,
and there weren't many passers-by,
which was just the way
Badger liked it.

"But it's too quiet for me!" said Bunny.

"If you like company, why not try
living by the river?" suggested Otter.
"There's always lots going on down here."
But Bunny only had to take one look at Otter's
houseboat to know that it wouldn't suit her.

"It's much too wet here for me!" she wailed.

"Hmmm, then what about the meadow where
Field Mouse lives?" suggested Otter.

Field Mouse seemed happy living in the meadow,
but no matter how hard she tried, Bunny
just could not get comfortable there.

For a start there was no shade anywhere
and when the sun beat down it was very hot!

And the pollen from the poppies was extremely
sneezy, and the corn-stalks were scratchy.

So that was no good either.

"What about Owl's house?" suggested Field Mouse.
Owl lived in the loft of the old barn.
It was certainly dry, and very clean,
but there was something wrong with it too.
"It's just too draughty," said Bunny.

Would she ever find
a new home?

By the mountain the little rabbit found an
empty cave. It was slightly gloomy, but at least there was
lots of space. She thought it might be just the place,
until she heard a grumbly, growly sort of sound.
Then she realised — it was Bear's house!

"And Bear snores too much," said Bunny.
"I couldn't possibly live near him!"

The Cave

Bunny was about to give up when she found
a smart blue door in the roots of a chestnut tree.
"This would be perfect!" said Bunny to herself.

But something seemed wrong.
The place had a funny smell —
a frightful, foxy sort of smell...
Suddenly, Bunny felt very afraid and she ran away,
as fast as she could.

Bunny ran and ran, past the barn and the field,
the river and the forest, all the way back to Bluebell Hill.
She ran up the hill, past the bluebells and straight in
through her own front door.

Bunny looked around her little burrow.
"It's not too hot or too wet. It's not too quiet or too noisy.
In fact, it's the perfect place for me!"

And so it was!

The Brave
Little Owl

Little Owl fluffs up his soft, furry feathers.

His bright, round eyes peep out of the nest.
Then he squeaks. He squeaks because
he is afraid of the dark outside.

The fox cubs laugh as t̶h̶[...]̶ow.
"Owls are meant to like night-time best," they tease.

"What a funny little owl!" laugh the squirrels.

"An odd little owl," giggle the moths.

"A very strange owl," agree the rabbits,
"to be frightened of the dark."

The Brave
Little Owl

Little Owl fluffs up his soft, furry feathers.

His bright, round eyes peep out of the nest.
Then he squeaks. He squeaks because
he is afraid of the dark outside.

The fox cubs laugh as they play below.
"Owls are meant to like night-time best," they tease.

"What a funny little owl!" laugh the squirrels.

"An odd little owl," giggle the moths.

"A very strange owl," agree the rabbits,
"to be frightened of the dark."

Bunny ran and ran, past the barn and the field,
the river and the forest, all the way back to Bluebell Hill.
She ran up the hill, past the bluebells and straight in
through her own front door.

Bunny looked around her little burrow.
"It's not too hot or too wet. It's not too quiet or too noisy.
In fact, it's the perfect place for me!"

And so it was!

Mother Owl tries to comfort Little Owl.
"Be brave, Little Owl," she says.
"Look at the stars. See how beautiful they are."

"Be brave, Little Owl. Look at the moon.
See how big and golden it is," says Father Owl.

But Little Owl buries his head under his wing.

It is time for Little Owl to learn to fly.
He sits on the branches of the tree with
the other baby owls in a wobbling row.
The breeze blows their feathers
and the leaves whisper.
The other forest creatures come to watch.

Little Owl is terrified. He closes his eyes.
Then, suddenly, he hears a night-bird singing.
The music is beautiful.

He hears a waterfall splashing.
The sound is exciting.

He wants to hear more and he forgets to be afraid.

Little Owl edges along the branch to hear better.
His eyes are still shut tight, so he does not see that
he has reached the end of the branch. . .

. . . WHOOSH!

Little Owl tumbles down in a blur of feathers.
Be brave, Little Owl!

Little Owl spreads his wings to try and balance.
The warm breeze scoops him up and holds him gently.
Little Owl flaps his wings. Little Owl is flying!
He opens his big, round eyes in amazement.

All the forest animals cheer!

Little Owl opens his big, round eyes even wider.
He flies above the forest.
He flies across the golden moon.
He flies past the sparkling, glittering stars.

Little Owl flies down and perches on his branch.

He looks out over the trees,
listening to the sounds of the forest creatures.

He looks out over the lake, which is
sparkling with reflections of the moon and stars.

Brave Little Owl sees that the night
is not so dark after all.

Brave Little Owl sees how bright the night is.
It is beautiful!
"Tu-whit tu-whoo," sings Brave Little Owl,
and he flies off into the shining, silver night.

PIPPBROOK BOOKS

First published as individual titles in the UK in 1999 by Templar Publishing
This treasury edition produced in 2014 by Pippbrook Books,
an imprint of the Templar Company Limited,
Deepdene Lodge, Deepdene Avenue, Dorking, Surrey, RH5 4AT, UK
www.templarco.co.uk

'The Blackberry Mouse'
Written by Matthew Grimsdale
Illustrated by Tony Linsell

'The Little Lost Duckling'
Written by Sue Barraclough
Illustrated by Simon Mendez

'The Bunny of Bluebell Hill'
Written by Tim Preston
Illustrated by Lorna Hussey

'The Brave Little Owl'
Written by Gill Davies
Illustrated by Dick Twinney

1 3 5 7 9 10 8 6 4 2

ISBN 978-1-78370-095-0

Designed by Hayley Bebb and Manhar Chauhan
Edited by Dugald Steer and Liza Miller

Printed in China